PUFFIN BOOKS

THE GIRAFFE AND THE PELLY AND ME

Roald Dahl's parents were Norwegian, but he was born in South Wales, in 1916, and educated at Repton School. He was a fighter pilot for the RAF during the Second World War, and it was writing about his experiences during this time that started his career as an author.

He is celebrated for his adult short stories as well as his fabulously popular children's books which have won many awards and are read by children all over the world. One of his earliest stories, *Charlie and the Chocolate Factory*, was voted the best children's book of all time. He spent most of his working life in Great Missenden, Buckinghamshire; an area of the countryside which features in many of his stories. He died in November 1990.

Quentin Blake was born in the suburbs of London in 1932. He read English at Cambridge, and did a postgraduate certificate in education at London University. From 1949 he worked as a cartoonist for many magazines, most notably *Punch* and *The Spectator*. He moved into children's book illustration where his inimitable style has won him enormous acclaim. Alongside this he has pursued a teaching career: he was head of the illustration department at the Royal College of Art and is now a visiting professor. Quentin Blake was awarded the OBE in 1987.

Other Books by Roald Dahl

James and the Giant Peach
Charlie and the Chocolate Factory
Fantastic Mr Fox
The Magic Finger
Charlie and the Great Glass Elevator
Danny, the Champion of the World
The Wonderful Story of Henry Sugar and Six More
The Enormous Crocodile
The Twits
George's Marvellous Medicine
Roald Dahl's Revolting Rhymes
The BFG
Dirty Beasts
The Witches
Boy
Going Solo
Matilda
Rhyme Stew
Esio Trot
The Minpins

Roald Dahl

The Giraffe and the Pelly and Me

Illustrated by Quentin Blake

PUFFIN BOOKS

For Neisha, Charlotte and Lorina

PUFFIN BOOKS

Published by the Penguin Group
Penguin Books Ltd, 27 Wrights Lane, London W8 5TZ, England
Penguin Books USA Inc., 375 Hudson Street, New York, New York 10014, USA
Penguin Books Australia Ltd, Ringwood, Victoria, Australia
Penguin Books Canada Ltd, 10 Alcorn Avenue, Toronto, Ontario, Canada M4V 3B2
Penguin Books (NZ) Ltd, 182–190 Wairau Road, Auckland 10, New Zealand

Penguin Books Ltd, Registered Offices: Harmondsworth, Middlesex, England

First published by Jonathan Cape 1985
This edition with new illustrations first published by Jonathan Cape 1992
Published in Puffin Books 1993
3 5 7 9 10 8 6 4 2

Text copyright © Roald Dahl, 1985
Illustrations copyright © Quentin Blake, 1992
All rights reserved

The moral right of the author has been asserted

Printed in England by Clays Ltd, St Ives plc

Not far from where I live there is a queer old empty wooden house standing all by itself on the side of the road. I long to explore inside it but the door is always locked, and when I peer through a window all I can see is darkness and dust. I know the ground floor used once to be a shop because I can still read the faded lettering across the front which says THE GRUBBER. My mother has told me that in our part of the country in the olden days a grubber was another name for a sweet-shop, and now every time I look at it I think to myself what a lovely old sweet-shop it must have been.

On the shop-window itself somebody has painted in white the words FOR SAIL.

One morning, I noticed that FOR SAIL had been scraped off the shop-window and in its place somebody had painted SOLED. I stood there staring at the new writing and wishing like mad that it had been me who had bought it because then I would have been able to make it into a grubber all over again. I have always longed and longed to own a sweet-shop. The sweet-shop of my dreams would be loaded from top to bottom with Sherbet Suckers and Caramel Fudge and

Russian Toffee and Sugar Snorters and Butter Gumballs and thousands and thousands of other glorious things like that. Oh boy, what I couldn't have done with that old Grubber shop if it had been mine!

On my next visit to The Grubber, I was standing across the road gazing at the wonderful old building when suddenly an enormous bathtub came sailing out through one of the second-floor windows and crashed right on to the middle of the road!

A few moments later, a white porcelain lavatory pan with the wooden seat still on it came flying out of the same window and landed with a wonderful splintering crash just beside the bathtub. This was followed by a kitchen sink and an empty canary-cage and a four-poster bed and two hot-water bottles and a rocking horse and a sewing-machine and goodness knows what else besides.

It looked as though some madman was ripping out the whole of the inside of the house, because now pieces of staircase and bits of the banisters and a whole lot of old floorboards came whistling through the windows.

Then there was silence. I waited and waited but not another sound came from within the building. I crossed the road and stood right under the windows and called out, "Is anybody at home?"

There was no answer.

In the end it began to get dark so I had to turn away and start walking home. But you can bet your life nothing was going to stop me from hurrying back there again tomorrow morning to see what the next surprise was going to be.

When I got back to the Grubber house the next morning, the first thing I noticed was the new door. The dirty old brown door had been taken out and in its place someone had fitted a brand-new red one. The new door was fantastic. It was twice as high as the other one had been and it looked ridiculous. I couldn't begin to imagine who would want a tremendous tall door like that in his house unless it was a giant.

As well as this, somebody had scraped away the SOLED notice on the shop-window and now there was a whole lot of different writing all over the glass. I stood there reading it and reading it and trying to figure out what on earth it all meant.

I tried to catch some sign or sound of movement inside the house but there was none . . . until all of a sudden . . . out of the corner of my eye . . . I noticed that one of the windows on the top floor was slowly beginning to open outwards . . .

Then a HEAD appeared at the open window.

I stared at the head. The head stared back at me with big round dark eyes.

Suddenly, a second window was flung wide open and of all the crazy things a gigantic white bird hopped out and perched on the window-sill. I knew what this

one was because of its amazing beak which was shaped like a huge orange-coloured basin. The Pelican looked down at me and sang out:

> *"Oh, how I wish*
> *For a big fat fish!*
> *I'm as hungry as ever could be!*
> *A dish of fish is my only wish!*
> *How far are we from the sea?"*

"We are a long way from the sea," I called back to him, "but there is a fishmonger in the village not far away."

"A fish *what*?"

"A fish*monger*."

"Now what on earth would that be?" asked the Pelican. "I have heard of a fish-*pie* and a fish-*cake* and a fish-*finger*, but I have never heard of a fish-*monger*. Are these mongers good to eat?"

This question baffled me a bit, so I said, "Who is your friend in the next window?"

"She is the Giraffe!" the Pelican answered. "Is she not wonderful? Her legs are on the ground floor and her head is looking out of the top window!"

As if all this wasn't enough, the window on the *first floor* was now flung wide open and out popped a Monkey!

The Monkey stood on the window-sill and did a jiggly little dance. He was so skinny he seemed to be made only out of furry bits of wire, but he danced wonderfully well, and I clapped and cheered and did a little dance myself in return.

"We are the Window-Cleaners!" sang out the Monkey.

"We will polish your glass
Till it's shining like brass
And it sparkles like sun on the sea!
We are quick and polite,
We will come day or night,
The Giraffe and the Pelly and me!

We're a fabulous crew,
We know just what to do,
And we never stop work to drink tea.
All your windows will glow
When we give them a go,
The Giraffe and the Pelly and me!

We use water and soap
Plus some kindness and hope,
But we never use ladders, not we.
Who needs ladders at all
When you're thirty feet tall?
Not Giraffe, and not Pelly! Not me!"

I stood there enthralled. Then I heard the Giraffe saying to the Pelican in the next window, "Pelly, my dear, be so good as to fly down and bring that small person up here to talk to us."

At once the Pelican spread his huge white wings and flew down on to the road beside me. "Hop in," he said, opening his enormous beak.

I stared at the great orange beak and backed away.

"Go ON!" the Monkey shouted from up in his window. "The Pelly isn't going to *swallow* you! Climb IN!"

I said to the Pelican, "I'll only get in if you promise not to shut your beak once I'm inside."

"You have nothing to fear!" cried the Pelican,

"And let me tell you why.
I have a very special beak!
A special beak have I!
You'll never see a beak so fine,
I don't care where you go.
There's magic in this beak of mine!
Hop in and don't say NO!"

"I will *not* hop in," I said, "unless you swear on your honour you won't shut it once I'm inside. I don't like small dark places."

"When I have done what I am just about to do," said the Pelican, "I won't be *able* to shut it. You don't seem to understand how my beak works."

"Show me," I said.

"Watch this!" cried the Pelican.

I watched in amazement as the top half of the Pelican's beak began to slide smoothly backwards into his head until the whole thing was almost out of sight.

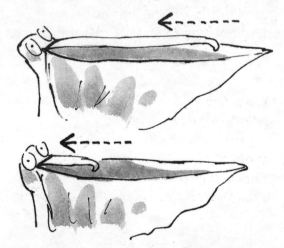

"It bends and goes down inside the back of my neck!" cried the Pelican. "Is that not sensible? Is it not magical?"

"It's unbelievable," I said. "It's exactly like one of those metal tape-measures my father's got at home. When it's out, it's straight. When you slide it back in, it bends and disappears."

"Precisely," said the Pelican. "You see, the top half is of no use to me unless I am chewing fish. The bottom half is what counts, my lad! The bottom half of this glorious beak of mine is the bucket in which we carry our window-cleaning water! So if I didn't slide the top half away I'd be standing around all day long holding it open!

> "So I slide it away
> For the rest of the day!
> Even so, I'm still able to speak!
> And wherever I've flown
> It has always been known
> As the Pelican's Patented Beak!

If I want to eat fish
(That's my favourite dish)
All I do is I give it a tweak!
In the blink of an eye
Out it pops! And they cry,
'It's the Pelican's Patented Beak!'"

"Stop showing off down there!" shouted the Monkey from the upstairs window. "Hurry up and bring that small person up to us! The Giraffe is waiting!"

I climbed into the big orange beak, and with a swoosh of wings the Pelican carried me back to his perch on the window-sill.

The Giraffe looked out of her window at me and said, "How do you do? What is your name?"

"Billy," I told her.

"Well, Billy," she said, "we need your help and we need it fast. We *must have* some windows to clean. We've spent every penny we had on buying this house and we've got to earn some more money quickly. The Pelly is starving, the Monkey is famished and I am perishing with hunger. The Pelly needs fish. The Monkey needs nuts and I am even more difficult to feed. I am a Geraneous Giraffe and a Geraneous Giraffe cannot eat anything except the pink and purple flowers of the tinkle-tinkle tree. But those, as I am sure you know, are hard to find and expensive to buy."

The Pelican cried out, "Right now I am so hungry I could eat a stale sardine!

> *"Has anyone seen a stale sardine*
> *Or a bucket of rotten cod?*
> *I'd eat the lot upon the spot,*
> *I'm such a hungry bod!"*

Every time the Pelican spoke, the beak I was standing in jiggled madly up and down, and the more excited he got, the more it jiggled.

The Monkey said, "What Pelly's *really* crazy about is salmon!"

"Yes, yes!" cried the Pelican. "Salmon! Oh, glorious salmon! I dream about it all day long but I never get any!"

"And *I* dream about walnuts!" shouted the Monkey. "A walnut fresh from the tree is scrumptious-galumptious, so flavory-savory, so sweet to eat that it makes me all wobbly just thinking about it!"

At exactly that moment, a huge white Rolls-Royce pulled up right below us, and a chauffeur in a blue and gold uniform got out. He was carrying an envelope in one gloved hand.

"Good heavens!" I whispered. "That's the Duke of Hampshire's car!"

"Who's he?" asked the Giraffe.

"He's the richest man in England!" I said.

The chauffeur knocked on the door of The Grubber.

He looked up and saw us. He saw the Giraffe, the Pelly, the Monkey and me all staring down at him from above, but not a muscle moved in his face, not an eyebrow was raised. The chauffeurs of very rich men are never surprised by anything they see. The chauffeur said, "His Grace The Duke of Hampshire has instructed me to deliver this envelope to The Ladderless Window-Cleaning Company."

"That's us!" cried the Monkey.

The Giraffe said, "Be so good as to open the envelope and read us the letter."

The chauffeur unfolded the letter and began to read, " 'Dear Sirs, I saw your notice as I drove by this morning. I have been looking for a decent window-cleaner for the last fifty years but I have not found one yet. My house has six hundred and seventy-seven windows in it (not counting the greenhouse) and all of them are filthy. Kindly come and see me as soon as possible. Yours truly, Hampshire.' That", added the chauffeur in a voice filled with awe and respect, "was written by His Grace The Duke of Hampshire in his own hand."

The Giraffe said to the chauffeur, "Please tell His Grace The Duke that we will be with him as soon as possible."

The chauffeur touched his cap and got back into the Rolls-Royce.

"Whoopee!" shouted the Monkey.

"Fantastic!" cried the Pelican. "That must be the best window-cleaning job in the world!"

"Billy," said the Giraffe, "what is the house called and how do we get there?"

"It is called Hampshire House," I said. "It's just over the hill. I'll show you the way."

"We're off!" cried the Monkey. "We're off to see the Duke!"

The Giraffe stooped low and went out through the tall door. The Monkey jumped off the window-sill on to the Giraffe's back. The Pelican, with me in his beak hanging on for dear life, flew across and perched on the very top of the Giraffe's head. And away we went.

It wasn't long before we came to the gates of Hampshire House, and as the Giraffe moved slowly up the great wide driveway, we all began to feel just a little bit nervous.

"What's he like, this Duke?" the Giraffe asked me.

"I don't know," I said. "But he's very very famous and very rich. People say he has twenty-five gardeners just to look after his flower-beds."

Soon the huge house itself came into view, and what a house it was! It was like a palace! It was bigger than a palace!

"Just look at those windows!" cried the Monkey. "They'll keep us going for ever!"

Then suddenly we heard a man's voice a short distance away to the right. "I want those big black ones at the top of the tree!" the man was shouting. "Get me those great big black ones!"

We peered round the bushes and saw an oldish man with an immense white moustache standing under a tall cherry tree and pointing his walking-stick in the air. There was a ladder against the tree and another man, who was probably a gardener, was up the ladder.

"Get me those great big black juicy ones right at the very top!" the old man was shouting.

"I can't reach them, Your Grace," the gardener called back. "The ladder isn't long enough!"

"Damnation!" shouted the Duke. "I *was* so looking forward to eating those big ones!"

"Here we go!" the Pelican whispered to me, and
with a swish and a swoop he carried me up to the very
top of the cherry tree and there he perched. "Pick
them, Billy!" he whispered. "Pick them quickly and
put them in my beak!"

The gardener got such a shock he fell off the ladder.
Down below us, the Duke was shouting, "My gun!
Get me my gun! Some damnable monster of a bird is
stealing my best cherries! Be off with you, sir! Go
away! Those are *my* cherries, not yours! I'll have you
shot for this, sir! Where *is* my gun?"

"Hurry, Billy!" whispered the Pelican. "Hurry,
hurry, hurry!"

"My gun!" the Duke was shouting to the gardener.
"Get me my gun, you idiot! I'll have that thieving bird
for breakfast, you see if I don't."

"I've picked them all," I whispered to the Pelican.

At once the Pelly flew down and landed right beside the furious figure of the Duke of Hampshire, who was prancing about and waving his stick in the air!

"Your cherries, Your Grace!" I said as I leaned over the edge of the Pelican's beak and offered a handful to the Duke.

The Duke was staggered. He reeled back and his eyes popped nearly out of their sockets. "Great Scott!" he gasped. "Good Lord! What's this? Who are *you*?"

And now the Giraffe, with the Monkey dancing about on her back, emerged suddenly from the bushes. The Duke stared at them. He looked as though he was about to have a fit.

"*Who are these creatures?*" he bellowed. "Has the whole world gone completely dotty?"

"We are the window-cleaners!" sang out the Monkey.

> "*We will polish your glass*
> *Till it's shining like brass*
> *And it sparkles like sun on the sea!*
> *We will work for Your Grace*
> *Till we're blue in the face,*
> *The Giraffe and the Pelly and me!*"

"You *asked* us to come and see you," the Giraffe said.

The truth was at last beginning to dawn on the Duke. He put a cherry into his mouth and chewed it slowly. Then he spat out the stone. "I like the way you picked these cherries for me," he said. "Could you also pick my apples in the autumn?"

"We could! We could! Of course we could!" we all shouted.

"And who are *you*?" the Duke said, pointing his stick at me.

"He is our Business Manager," the Giraffe said. "His name is Billy. We go nowhere without him."

"Very well, very well," the Duke muttered. "Come along with me and let's see if you're any good at cleaning windows."

I climbed out of the Pelican's beak and the kindly old Duke took me by the hand as we all walked towards the house. When we got there, the Duke said, "What happens next?"

"It is all very simple, Your Grace," the Giraffe replied. "I am the ladder, the Pelly is the bucket and the Monkey is the cleaner. Watch us go!"

With that, the famous window-cleaning gang sprang into action. The Monkey jumped down from the Giraffe's back and turned on the garden tap. The Pelican held his great beak under the tap until it was full of water. Then, with a wonderful springy leap the Monkey leaped up once again on to the Giraffe's back.

From there he scrambled, as easily as if he were climbing a tree, up the long long neck of the Giraffe until he stood balancing on the very top of her head. The Pelican remained standing on the ground beside us, looking up at the Giraffe.

"We'll do the top floor first!" the Giraffe shouted down. "Bring the water up, please."

The Duke called out, "Don't worry about the two top floors. You can't reach them anyway."

"Who says we can't reach them?" the Giraffe called back.

"I do," the Duke said firmly, "And I'm not having any of you risking your silly necks around here."

If you wish to be friends with a Giraffe, never say anything bad about its neck. Its neck is its proudest possession.

"What's wrong with my neck?" snapped the Giraffe.

"Don't argue with me, you foolish creature!" cried the Duke. "If you can't reach it, you can't reach it and that's the end of it! Now get on with your work!"

"Your Grace," the Giraffe said, giving the Duke a small superior smile, "there are no windows in the world I cannot reach with this magical neck of mine."

The Monkey, who was dancing about most dangerously on top of the Giraffe's head, cried out, "Show him, Giraffey! Go on and show him what you can do with your magical neck!"

The next moment, the Giraffe's neck, which heaven knows was long enough already, began to grow longer and L O N G E R

and L O N G E R

and L O N G E R

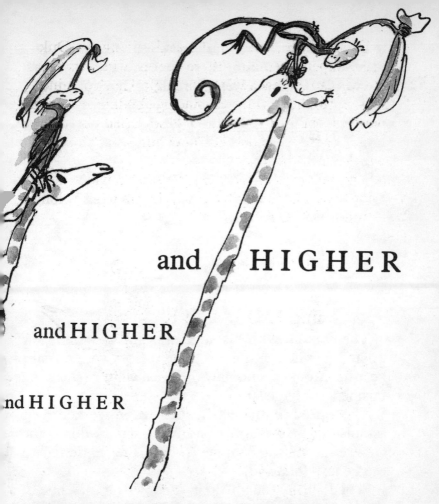

and **HIGHER**

and **HIGHER**

nd **HIGHER**

until at last the Giraffe's head with the Monkey on top of it was level with the windows of the top floor.

The Giraffe looked down from her great height and said to the Duke, "How's that?"

The Duke was speechless. So was I. It was the most magical thing I had ever seen, more magical even than the Pelican's Patented Beak.

Up above us, the Giraffe was beginning to sing a little song, but she sang so softly I could hardly catch the words. I think it went something like this:

"My neck can stretch terribly high,
Much higher than eagles can fly.
If I ventured to show
Just how high it would go
You'd lose sight of my head in the sky!"

The Pelican, with his huge beak full of water, flew up and perched on one of the top-floor window-sills near the Monkey, and now the great window-cleaning business really began.

The speed with which the team worked was astonishing. As soon as one window was done, the Giraffe moved the Monkey over to the next one and the Pelican followed.

When all the fourth-floor windows on that side of the house were finished, the Giraffe simply drew in her magical neck until the Monkey was level with the third-floor windows and off they went again.

"Amazing!" cried the Duke. "Astonishing! Remarkable! Incredible! I haven't seen out of any of my windows for forty years! Now I shall be able to sit indoors and enjoy the view!"

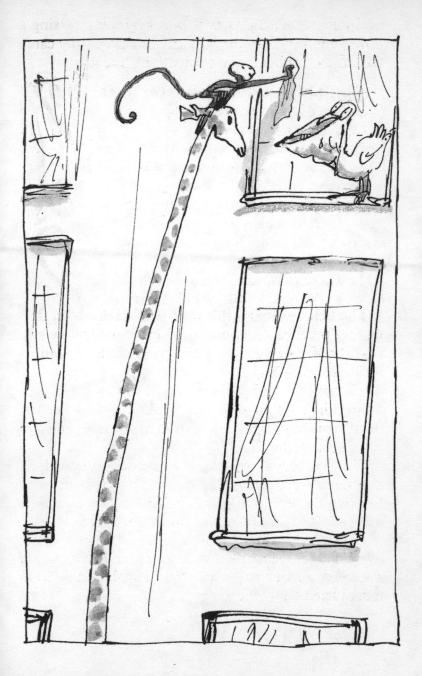

Suddenly I saw all three of the Window-Cleaners stop dead in their tracks. They seemed to freeze against the wall of the house. None of them moved.

"What's happened to them?" the Duke asked me. "What's gone wrong?"

"I don't know," I answered.

Then the Giraffe, with the Monkey on her head, tiptoed very gingerly away from the house and came towards us. The Pelican flew with them. The Giraffe came up very close to the Duke and whispered, "Your Grace, there is a man in one of the bedrooms on the third floor. He is opening all the drawers and taking things out. He's got a pistol!"

The Duke jumped about a foot in the air. "Which room?" he snapped. "Show me at once!"

"It's the one on the third floor where the window is wide open," the Giraffe whispered.

"By Gad!" cried the Duke. "That's the Duchess's bedroom! He's after her jewels! Call the police! Summon the army! Bring up the cannon! Charge with the Light Brigade!" But even as he spoke the Pelican was flying up into the air. As he flew, he turned himself upside-down and tipped the window-cleaning water out of his beak. Then I saw the top half of that marvellous patented beak sliding out of his head, ready for action.

"What's that crazy bird up to?" cried the Duke.

"Wait and see," shouted the Monkey. "Hold your breath, old man! Hold your nose! Hold your horses and watch the Pelly go!"

Like a bullet the Pelican flew in through the open-window, and five seconds later out he came again with his great orange beak firmly closed. He landed on the lawn beside the Duke.

A tremendous banging noise was coming from inside the Pelican's beak. It sounded as though someone was using a sledgehammer against it from the inside.

"He's got him!" cried the Monkey. "Pelly's got the burglar in his beak!"

"Well done, sir!" shouted the Duke, hopping about with excitement. Suddenly he pulled the handle of his walking-stick upwards, and out of the hollow inside of the stick itself he drew a long thin sharp shining sword. "I'll run him through!" he shouted, flourishing the sword like a fencer. "Open up, Pelican! Let me get at him! I'll run the bounder through before he knows what's happened to him! I'll spike him like a pat of butter! I'll feed his gizzards to my foxhounds!"

But the Pelican did not open his beak. He kept it firmly closed and shook his head at the Duke.

The Giraffe shouted, "The burglar is armed with a pistol, Your Grace! If Pelly lets him out now he'll shoot us all!"

"He can be armed with a *machine-gun* for all I care!" bellowed the Duke, his massive moustaches bristling like brushwood. "I'll handle the blighter! Open up, sir! Open up!"

Suddenly there was an ear-splitting BANG and the Pelican leaped twenty feet into the air. So did the Duke.

"Watch out!" the Duke shouted, taking ten rapid paces backwards. "He's trying to shoot his way out!" And pointing his sword at the Pelican, he bellowed, "Keep that beak closed, sir! Don't you dare let him out! He'll murder us all!"

"Shake him up, Pelly!" cried the Giraffe. "Rattle his bones! Teach him not to do it again!"

The Pelican shook his head so fast from side to side that the beak became a blur and the man inside must have felt he was being scrambled like eggs.

"Well done, Pelly!" cried the Giraffe. "You're doing a great job! Keep on shaking him so he doesn't fire that pistol again!"

At this point, a lady with an enormous chest and flaming orange hair came flying out of the house screaming, "My jewels! Somebody's stolen my jewels! My diamond tiara! My diamond necklace! My diamond bracelets! My diamond earrings! My diamond rings! They've had the lot! My rooms have been ransacked!"

And then this massive female, who fifty-five years ago had been a world-famous opera-singer, suddenly burst into song.

> "My diamonds are over the ocean,
> My diamonds are over the sea,
> My diamonds were pinched from my bedroom,
> Oh, bring back my diamonds to me."

We were so bowled over by the power of the lady's lungs that all of us, excepting the Pelican, who had to keep his beak closed, joined in the chorus.

"*Bring back, bring back,*
Oh, bring back my diamonds to me, to me.
Bring back, bring back,
Oh, bring back my diamonds to me!"

"Calm yourself, Henrietta," said the Duke. He pointed to the Pelican and said, "This clever bird, this brilliant burglar-catching creature has saved the day! The bounder's in his beak!"

The Duchess stared at the Pelican. The Pelican stared back at the Duchess and gave her a wink.

"If he's in there," cried the Duchess, "why don't you let him out! Then you can run him through with that famous sword of yours! I want my diamonds! Open your beak, bird!"

"No, no!" shouted the Duke. "He's got a pistol! He'll murder us all!"

Someone must have called the police because suddenly no less than four squad cars came racing towards us with their sirens screaming.

Within seconds we were surrounded by six policemen, and the Duke was shouting to them, "The villain you are after is inside the beak of that bird! Stand by to collar him!" And to the Pelican he said, "Get ready to open up! Are you ready ... steady ... *go*! Open her up!"

The Pelican opened his gigantic beak and immediately the policemen pounced upon the burglar who was crouching inside. They snatched his pistol away from him and dragged him out and put handcuffs on his wrists.

"Great Scott!" shouted the Chief of Police. "It's the Cobra himself!"

"The who! The what!" everyone asked. "Who's the Cobra?"

"The Cobra is the cleverest and most dangerous catburglar in the world!" said the Chief of Police. "He must have climbed up the drainpipe. The Cobra can climb up anything!"

"My diamonds!" screamed the Duchess. "I want my diamonds! Where are my diamonds?"

"Here they are!" cried the Chief of Police, fishing great handfuls of jewellery from the burglar's pockets.

The Duchess was so overcome with relief that she fell to the ground in a faint.

When the police had taken away the fearsome burglar known as the Cobra, and the fainting Duchess had been carried into the house by her servants, the old Duke stood on the lawn with the Giraffe, the Pelican, the Monkey and me.

"Look!" cried the Monkey. "That rotten burglar's bullet has made a hole in poor Pelly's beak!"

"That's done it," said the Pelican. "Now it won't be any use for holding water when we clean the windows."

"Don't you worry about that, my dear Pelly," said the Duke, patting him on the beak. "My chauffeur will soon put a patch over it the same way he mends the tyres on the Rolls. Right now we have far more important things to talk about than a little hole in a beak."

We stood there waiting to see what the Duke was going to say next.

"Now listen to me, all of you," he said. "Those diamonds were worth millions! Millions and millions! and *you* have saved them!"

The Monkey nodded. The Giraffe smiled. The Pelican blushed.

"No reward is too great for you," the Duke went on. "I am therefore going to make you an offer which I hope will give you pleasure. I hereby invite the Giraffe and the Pelican and the Monkey to live on my estate for the rest of their lives.

"I shall give you my best and largest hay-barn as your private house. Central heating, showers, a kitchen and anything else you desire for your comfort will be installed.

"In return, you will keep my windows clean, and pick my cherries and my apples. If the Pelican is willing, perhaps he will also give me a ride in his beak now and again."

"A pleasure, Your Grace!" cried the Pelican. "Would you like a ride now?"

"Later," said the Duke. "I'll have one after tea."

At this point, the Giraffe gave a nervous little cough and looked up at the sky.

"Is there a problem?" asked the Duke. "If there is, do please let me hear it."

"I don't like to sound ungrateful or pushy," murmured the Giraffe, "but we do have one very pressing problem. We are all absolutely famished. We haven't eaten for days."

"My *dear* Giraffey!" cried the Duke. "How very thoughtless of me. Food is no problem around here."

"I'm afraid it is not quite as easy as all that," said the Giraffe. "You see, I myself happen to be ..."

"Don't tell me!" cried the Duke. "I know it already! I am an expert on the animals of Africa. The moment I saw you I knew you were no ordinary giraffe. You are of the Geraneous variety, are you not?"

"You are absolutely right, Your Grace," said the Giraffe. "But the trouble with us is that we only eat ..."

"You don't have to tell me that either!" cried the Duke. "I know perfectly well a Geraneous Giraffe can eat only one kind of food. Am I not right in thinking that the pink and purple flowers of the tinkle-tinkle tree are your only diet?"

"Yes," sighed the Giraffe, "and that's been my problem ever since I arrived on these shores."

"That is no problem at all here at Hampshire House," said the Duke. "Look over there, my dear Giraffey, and you will see the only plantation of tinkle-tinkle trees in the entire country!"

The Giraffe looked. She gave a gasp of astonishment, and at first she was so overwhelmed she couldn't even speak. Great tears of joy began running down her cheeks.

"Help yourself," said the Duke. "Eat all you want."

"Oh, my sainted souls!" gasped the Giraffe. "Oh, my naked neck! I cannot *believe* what I am seeing!"

The next moment she was galloping full speed across the lawns and whinnying with excitement and the last we saw of her, she was burying her head in the beautiful pink and purple flowers that blossomed on the tops of the trees all around her.

"As for the Monkey," the Duke went on, "I think he also will be pleased with what I have to offer. All over my estate there are thousands of giant nut trees ..."

"Nuts?" cried the Monkey. "What kind of nuts?"

"Walnuts, of course," said the Duke.

"*Walnuts!*" screamed the Monkey. "Not *walnuts*? You don't really mean *walnuts*? You're pulling my leg! You're joking! You can't be serious! I must have heard wrong!"

"There's a walnut tree right over there," the Duke said, pointing.

The Monkey took off like an arrow, and a few seconds later he was high up in the branches of the walnut tree, cracking the nuts and guzzling what was inside.

"That leaves only the Pelly," said the Duke.

"Yes," said the Pelican nervously, "but I'm afraid that what I eat does not grow on trees. I only eat fish. Would it be too much trouble, I wonder, if I were to ask you for a reasonably fresh piece of haddock or cod every day?"

"Haddock or cod!" shouted the Duke, spitting out the words as though they made a bad taste in his mouth. "Cast your eyes, my dear Pelly, over there to the south."

The Pelican looked across the vast rolling estate and in the distance he saw a great river.

"That is the River Hamp!" cried the Duke. "The finest salmon river in the whole of Europe!"

"*Salmon!*" screeched the Pelican. "Not *salmon*? You don't really mean *salmon*?"

"It's *full* of salmon," the Duke said, "and I own it.
You can help yourself."

Before he had finished speaking the Pelican was in
the air. The Duke and I watched him as he flew full
speed towards the river. We saw him circle over the
water, then he dived and disappeared. A few moments
later, he was in the air again, and he had a gigantic
salmon in his beak.

I stood alone with the Duke on the lawn beside his great house. "Well, Billy," he said, "I'm glad they are all happy. But what about you, my lad? I am wondering if you happen to have just one extra special little wish all for yourself. If you do, I'd love you to tell me about it."

There was a sudden tingling in my toes. It felt as though something tremendous might be going to happen to me any moment.

"Yes," I murmured nervously. "I do have one extra special little wish."

"And what might that be?" said the Duke in a kindly voice.

"There is an old wooden house near where I live," I said. "It's called The Grubber and long ago it used to be a sweet-shop. I have wished and wished that one day somebody might come along and make it into a marvellous new sweet-shop all over again."

"Somebody?" cried the Duke. "What do you mean, *somebody?*" You and I will do that! We'll do it together! We'll make it into the most wonderful sweet-shop in the world! And *you*, my boy, will own it!"

Whenever the old Duke got excited, his enormous moustaches started to bristle and jump about. Right now they were jumping up and down so much it looked as though he had a squirrel on his face. "By Gad, sir!" he cried, waving his stick, "I shall buy the place today! Then we'll all get to work and have the whole thing ready in no time! You just wait and see what sort of a sweet-shop we are going to make out of this Grubber place of yours!"

It was amazing how quickly things began to happen after that. There was no problem about buying the house because it was owned by the Giraffe and the Pelly and the Monkey, and they insisted upon giving it to the Duke for nothing.

Then builders and carpenters moved in and rebuilt the whole of the inside so that once again it had three floors. On all these floors they put together rows and rows of tall shelves, and there were ladders to climb up to the highest shelves and baskets to carry what you bought.

Then the sweets and chocs and toffees and fudges and nougats began pouring in to fill the shelves. They came by aeroplane from every country in the world, the most wild and wondrous things you could ever imagine.

There were Gumtwizzlers and Fizzwinkles from China, Frothblowers and Spitsizzlers from Africa, Tummyticklers and Gobwangles from the Fiji Islands and Liplickers and Plushnuggets from the Land of the Midnight Sun.

For two whole weeks the flood of boxes and sacks continued to arrive. I could no longer keep track of all the countries they came from, but you can bet your life that as I unpacked each new batch I sampled it carefully. I can remember especially the Giant Wangdoodles from Australia, every one with a huge ripe red strawberry hidden inside its crispy chocolate crust . . .

and the Electric Fizzcocklers
that made every hair on your
head stand straight up on
end as soon as you popped
one into your mouth . . . and
there were Nishnobblers and
Gumglotters and Blue
Bubblers and Sherbet Slur-
pers and Tongue Rakers,
and as well as all this, there
was a whole lot of splendid
stuff from the great Wonka
factory itself, for example
the famous Willy Wonka
Rainbow Drops – suck them
and you can spit in seven

different colours. And his
Stickjaw for talkative
parents. And his Mint
Jujubes that will give the boy
next door green teeth for a
month.

On the Grand Opening Day, I decided to allow all my customers to help themselves for free, and the place was so crowded with children you could hardly move. The television cameras and the newspaper reporters were all there, and the old Duke himself stood outside in the road with my friends the Giraffe and the Pelly and the Monkey watching the marvellous scene. I came out of the shop to join them for a few moments and I brought each of them a bag of extra special sweets as a present.

To the Duke, because the weather was a little chilly, I gave some Scarlet Scorchdroppers that had been sent to me from Iceland. The label said that they were guaranteed to make the person who sucked them as warm as toast even if he were standing stark naked at the North Pole in mid-winter. The moment the Duke popped one into his mouth, thick smoke came gushing out of the old boy's nostrils in such quantities that I thought his moustaches were going up in flames.

"Terrific!" he cried, hopping about. "Tremendous stuff! I'll take a case of them home with me!"

To the Giraffe I gave a bag of Glumptious Globgobblers. The Globgobbler is an especially delicious sweet that is made somewhere near Mecca, and the moment you bite into it, all the perfumed juices of Arabia go squirting down your gullet one after the other.

"It's wonderful!" cried the Giraffe as a cascade of lovely liquid flavours poured all the way down her long long throat. "It's even better than my favourite pink and purple flowers!"

To the Pelican I gave a big bag of Pishlets. Pishlets, as you probably know, are bought by children who are unable to whistle a tune as they walk along the street but long to do so. They had a splendid effect upon the Pelican, for after he had put one of them into his beak and chewed it for a while, he suddenly started singing like a nightingale. This made him wildly excited because Pelicans are not song-birds. No Pelican had ever been known to whistle a tune before.

To the Monkey I gave bag of Devil's Drenchers, those small fiery black sweets that one is not allowed to sell to children under four years old. When you have sucked a Devil's Drencher for a minute or so, you can set your breath alight and blow a huge column of fire twenty feet into the air. The Duke put a match to the Monkey's breath and shouted, "Blow, Monkey, blow!" A sheet of orange flame shot up as high as the roof of the Grubber house and it was wonderful.

"I've got to leave you now," I said. "I must go and look after my customers in the shop."

"We must go, too," said the Giraffe. "We have one hundred windows to clean before dark."

I said goodbye to the Duke, and then one by one I said goodbye to the three best friends I had ever had. Suddenly, we all became very quiet and melancholy, and the Monkey looked as though he was about to cry as he sang me a little song of farewell:

> *"We have tears in our eyes*
> *As we wave our goodbyes,*
> *We so loved being with you, we three.*
> *So do please now and then*
> *Come and see us again,*
> *The Giraffe and the Pelly and me.*
>
> *All you do is to look*
> *At a page in this book*
> *Because that's where we always will be.*
> *No book ever ends*
> *When it's full of your friends*
> *The Giraffe and the Pelly and me."*